For my gorgeous nephews (Fin, Lorcan, Jude, Arthur, Henry and Charlie)
and a huge thank you to Ashling, Emma, Dave, Mum and Dad for being
there for me no matter what. – C.C.

To Neve and Alex, always. – S.D.

First published in Great Britain 2021 by Farshore

An imprint of HarperCollins*Publishers*
1 London Bridge Street, London SE1 9GF
www.farshorebooks.com

HarperCollins*Publishers*
1st Floor, Watermarque Building, Ringsend Road
Dublin 4, Ireland

Text copyright © Claire Cashmore 2021
Illustrations copyright © Sharon Davey 2021
Claire Cashmore and Sharon Davey have asserted their moral rights.

ISBN 978 0 7555 0285 1
Printed in Italy
1

A CIP catalogue record for this title is available from the British Library.

Claire Cashmore Photo by Buda Mendes/Getty Images

SPLASH

Claire Cashmore

Illustrated by Sharon Davey

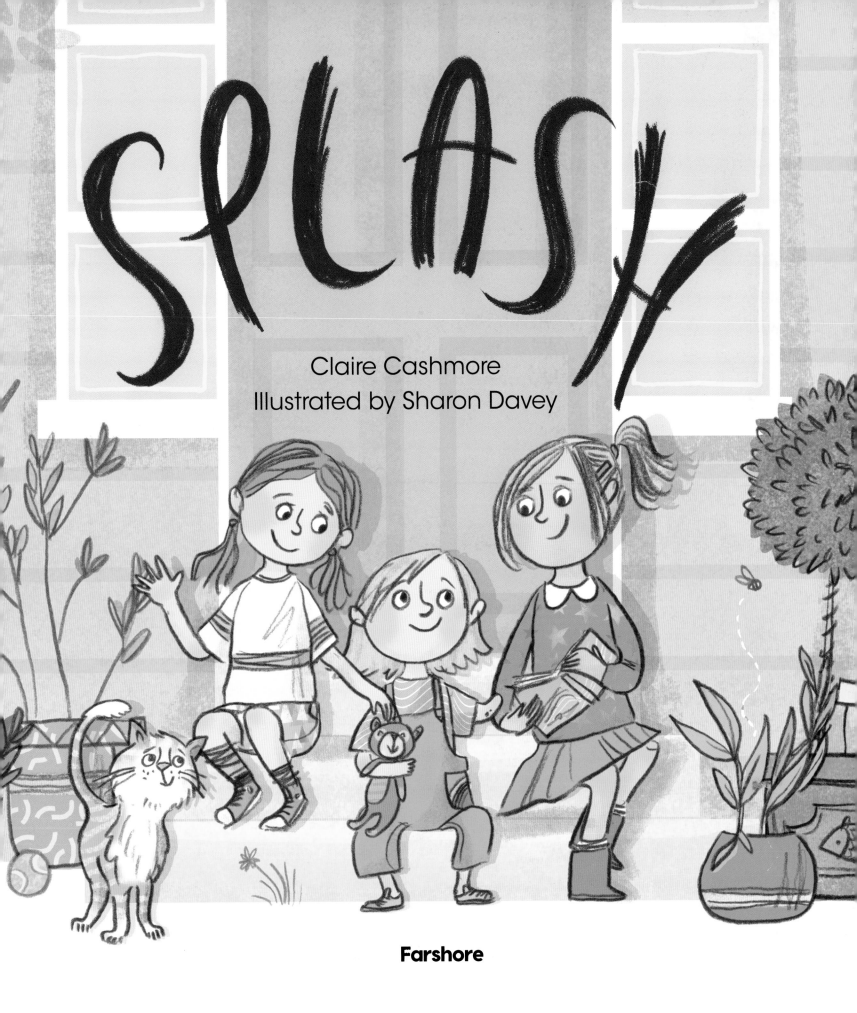

Farshore

This is Claire.

And these are Claire's big sisters. They call her Bear and ruffle her hair.

And whatever Claire's sisters can do, Claire can do too . . .

Like dressing up as kings and queens,

making castles out of boxes.

Like cartwheeling round the garden . . .

and spotting shooting stars,

perfect for dreaming big dreams.
There is nothing Claire can't do!

Wait, there is just *one thing*
Claire won't do . . .

The water in the pool makes
her feel squirmy inside.

Follow her sisters?
No, thank you!
Not today.

She'd rather pick up a SPIDER.

Eat a PICKLE sandwich.

Or even be chased by
a BEAR – *a real one!* –

than go near the
swirly, squirmy water.

But one hot day,
hot enough to melt
ice cream, Claire dares –

just enough to dip
one toe.

It sends a shiver down
her spine, so nice she
forgets that she's afraid.

She dips another toe,
then a foot . . .

Then a leg . . .

and finally . . .

With a shower of spray and a very loud squeal, **she is IN!**

She gasps and gulps and splashes and squeals. It feels . . .

AMAZING!

The water's like a silky blanket. Her reflection dances on the shimmering surface and bubbles pop between her fingers and toes.

Conquering her fear makes her feel like a superhero.

"Well done, Bear!" say her sisters and ruffle her hair.

And now she is in the water,
Claire won't get out.

She's splashing

and kicking

and floating

and gliding

and twisting

and flipping

and plunging.

In the pool, she feels invincible.
And she has a new dream . . .

Dressed in her best red swimsuit, Claire practises hard.

She swims metres.

Then kilometres.

Sometimes she's swift and strong . . .

Sometimes it's all too much.

But whatever she can't do today . . .

...she will conquer tomorrow!

And eventually she is ready to swim her very first race.
Proud as a lion, Claire prepares to dive.

THREE,

TWO,

ONE . . .

The whistles blows.

And she's away like a rocket, racing for gold . . .
Swinging and kicking. Bold and determined.
Her heart pounding like drums.

She slams her hand on
the side of the pool.

She's done it!

"Well done, Bear!" say her
sisters and ruffle her hair.

There are hugs and grins,
fist bumps and high fives.

Up on the podium, Claire grins from ear to ear. She throws her arms in the air and waves her stump with pride.

With a gold medal around her neck, her dreams are **bigger than ever.**

Because whatever she can't do today . . .

. . . she knows she will conquer tomorrow!

CLAIRE CASHMORE

PARALYMPICS GB GOLD MEDALLIST

CLAIRE CASHMORE MBE is a Paralympic swimming gold medallist. She has swum four times at the Paralympic Games, which are held every four years. Claire was just sixteen when she first competed at the Games. She felt so proud to step onto the podium with tens of thousands of people watching in the stadium and on TV! Since then, Claire has won eight Paralympic medals, including a gold at the 2016 Games in Rio. She now competes as a paratriathlete, running, cycling AND swimming. Three sports in one – that's seriously hard work! When she isn't training and competing, Claire spends her time encouraging disabled children and adults to get involved with sport. We can all do amazing things when we work hard and believe in ourselves . . . and Claire wants everyone to find their special way to shine!